Happy Days for Mouse and Mole
published by Graffeg in 2019.
Copyright © Graffeg Limited 2019.

PRINTING HISTORY
Picture Corgi edition published 1996.

Text copyright © Joyce Dunbar, Illustrations
copyright © James Mayhew, design and
production Graffeg Limited. This publication
and content is protected by copyright © 2019.

Joyce Dunbar and James Mayhew are hereby
identified as the authors of this work in
accordance with section 77 of the Copyrights,
Designs and Patents Act 1988.

A CIP Catalogue record for this book is
available from the British Library.

ISBN 9781912050383

1 2 3 4 5 6 7 8 9

Happy Days for
MOUSE & MOLE

Joyce Dunbar and James Mayhew

This book belongs to:

GRAFFEG

For Alison de Vere, with thanks
~ J.D and J.M ~

Contents

The Hammock

Mouse found a large piece of net. He tied one end to
the branch of a tree and the other end to a fence post.
　'This will make a very good hammock,' said Mouse
to himself.

Mole came to see what he was doing.

'That makes a very good hammock,' Mole said.

'That's what I thought,' said Mouse. 'Now I am going
to lie on my hammock and look at the sky through the
leaves and listen to the singing of the birds.'

'And let the breeze rock you gently to and fro,' said Mole.

'That's right,' said Mouse.

He was about to get into the hammock when Mole said, 'Wait a minute, Mouse!'

'What for?' asked Mouse.

'It doesn't look safe to me.'

'Why not?' asked Mouse.

'You never know what might happen. A branch might break off the tree and fall on your head.'

'I don't think so,' said Mouse, starting to climb into his hammock.

'But Mouse,' said Mole, 'the birds might sing too loudly and give you a headache.'

'I like birdsong,' said Mouse, trying once more to get into the hammock.

'The breeze might rock you too much and make you feel dizzy,' said Mole.

'The breeze will rock me just right,' said Mouse, still trying to get into his hammock.

'No, Mouse, I can't let you do it. I, Mole, will test it for you. I'll make sure it really is safe.' And, pushing Mouse out of the way, Mole clambered into the hammock.

'Aaah!' sighed Mole, stretching out and closing his eyes.

'How does it feel, Mole?' asked Mouse.

'Terrible,' said Mole. 'What you need to make this hammock comfortable is a cushion or two. Will you go and fetch them, Mouse?'

So Mouse went and got two cushions. He gave them to Mole.

'How does it feel now, Mole?' asked Mouse.

'Awful,' said Mole. 'Perhaps a jar of biscuits would make it all right. Will you bring a jar of biscuits, Mouse?'

So Mouse fetched a jar of biscuits for Mole.

'How is that now, Mole?' asked Mouse.

'Hmmm,' said Mole, munching one of the biscuits. 'The breeze isn't too strong. The birds are not singing too loudly. The branches are not falling from the tree. But to make it really perfect, you need some fresh lemonade to go with the biscuits. Would you go and make some, Mouse?'

So Mouse made some fresh lemonade.

'There you are, Mole!' he said. 'Two cushions. A jar of biscuits. Some fresh lemonade. Now you have made sure the hammock is really safe and comfortable. Thank you, Mole.'

'Oh, I am not really sure,' said Mole, sipping the lemonade. 'To make really sure, I need to test it for a good long time. I need to be left all alone. Now, you just pass me more biscuits and lemonade and leave me for a while.'

Mouse passed more biscuits and lemonade. Mole settled himself down. 'Bliss!' he sighed. 'Such bliss!'

But no sooner had he said these words than the hammock broke.

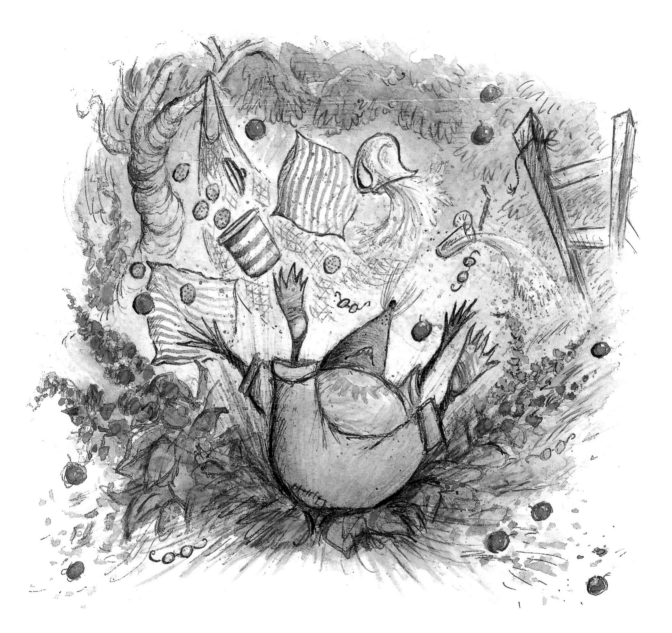

Mole went crashing to the ground and the biscuits and lemonade went flying. Mole was too astonished to speak.

'Why, Mole!' said Mouse. 'You were right. The hammock wasn't safe after all. You saved me a nasty bump. What a good friend you are! But I'll fix it properly this time. Now, you just rest on the cushions. And don't bother about lemonade and biscuits for me. I'll be happy with just the hammock.'

And Mouse was.

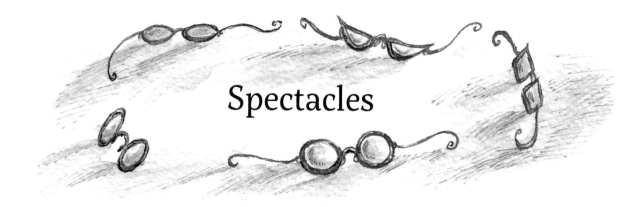

Spectacles

'I've lost my glasses,' said Mole.

'Which pair?' asked Mouse.

'The pair I need to find my other pairs of glasses,' said Mole.

Mouse lifted the cushion from Mole's armchair and groped around down the sides. He fished out a bent pair of spectacles. 'This pair?' he asked.

Mole tried them on. He peered dimly at Mouse.

'No,' said Mole, pushing the glasses up onto his head.

'Not this pair.'

Mouse got down on all fours and felt under the kitchen dresser. He pulled out another pair of spectacles. 'This pair?' he asked.

Mole put them on. He blinked blearily around the room.

'No,' said Mole, pushing the glasses up in front of the others. 'Not this pair either.'

Mouse went into the bedroom and gave the bedclothes a good shake. Out fell another pair of spectacles. 'This pair?' he asked.

Mole put them on and stumbled out into the hall. He bumped his snout against the bannister so that the glasses got pushed up with the others.

'No,' said Mole. 'Definitely not this pair.'

Mouse searched in the sock drawer. He looked along the cup hooks. He rummaged in the store cupboard. He brought out more and more glasses. Mole tried them on, one after the other, until the top of his head was crowned with a row of shining spectacles.

Mouse was feeling fed up. 'Mole,' he said. 'Why do you need so many pairs of glasses?'

'Why?' said Mole, twirling a pair of spectacles. 'Why?'

'Yes, why?'

'Well, I need glasses to wear, and glasses to spare.

I need glasses for the dark,

and glasses for the light...

I need glasses for things that are red,

and glasses for things that are green...

I need glasses for things that are small,

and glasses for things that are large...

I need glasses for things that are near, and glasses for things that are far...

18

I need glasses for things that I want to remember,

and glasses for things I want to forget...

I need glasses for things that are real,

and glasses for things I imagine...

I need glasses for things that make me sad,

and glasses for things that make me happy...

I need glasses to see my dear friend Mouse,

and I need glasses to find lost glasses, and...

'And a dear friend Mouse to find those glasses!'
interrupted Mouse from the laundry basket. 'And it must
be this pair,' he added, 'for there is nowhere else to look.'

Mole put them on. He stared happily around the room.
'Yes, this is the pair,' he exclaimed. 'My glasses for
finding other glasses!'

He began to search around.

He scrabbled through the sock drawer.

He looked along the cup hooks.

He hunted in the store cupboard. But he didn't find a single pair of spectacles.

'Mouse, this is serious,' he said. 'I *still* can't find my other glasses.'

'Mole,' said Mouse.

'What is it?' said Mole.

'Which pair do you use to look at yourself?'

'My best pair, of course, with tortoiseshell frames.'

'This pair?' said Mouse, moving them to the front of the row and leading Mole to the mirror.

Mole saw the row of glasses on his head. 'Why, Mouse!' he said. 'If only I had as many pairs of eyes, I'd be able to see everything at once!'

Catch a Falling Leaf

It was a misty autumn morning. The leaves were beginning to fall.

'Look, Mouse,' said Mole. 'The leaves are falling already.'

'You know what they say,' said Mouse. 'If you can catch a falling leaf, you will be lucky for the rest of the year.'

'Let's try,' said Mole.

'We will have a better chance in the wood,' said Mouse. 'It is full of leaves and trees.'

They were soon on their way through the wood. A breeze through the trees sent down some leaves in a flurry.
Mouse and Mole tried to catch one, running around with outstretched paws.

'Missed!' said Mouse.

'Missed!' said Mole.

'Missed again!' said Mouse.

'So did I,' said Mole.

The leaves kept falling and falling. Mouse and Mole kept trying and trying. Every time they missed.

They sat down on a tree stump for a rest.

'It's not as easy as it looks,' said Mouse.

'We need to be scientific,' said Mole. 'You see, the leaves are not falling straight down. They spin this way and that, they whirl and they twirl. Perhaps if we also spin this way and that, whirl and twirl, we will be able to catch a falling leaf.'

That moment, Mole spied a single falling leaf.
'Just watch,' said Mole. 'And I'll show you.'

The leaf danced round through
the air. Mole danced down on
the ground.

The leaf spun this way and that.
Mole spun that way and this.

The leaf whirled and twirled.
Mole twirled and whirled, while Mouse sat still and
looked on.

'Here it comes,' said Mole, doing a final pirouette. But just as the leaf seemed about to fall into his paw, Mole tripped over a branch...

stumbled over a hillock...

rolled down a bank...

bounced over a grassy hummock...

until he landed in a prickly bramble bush.

The leaf Mole was trying to catch landed straight in Mouse's lap.

'Are you all right, Mole?' called Mouse.

Only Mole's snout could be seen, and a paw that clutched a brown leaf. 'Look, Mouse!' he yelled. 'See what I have in my paw. It wasn't the one I was chasing, but it's a falling leaf just the same.'

'I'm sure one leaf is as good as another,' said Mouse, dropping his own leaf to the floor. 'Here, let me help you out of that bush.'

'What about you, Mouse? Did you manage to catch a leaf?'

'No, Mole, I didn't. I can't do a leaf dance like yours.'

'Oooh,' moaned Mole. 'I am scratched and stung all over.'

'Never mind,' said Mouse. 'You have proved you are a scientific mole.'

'I have,' said Mole.

'And you will be lucky for the rest of the year,' added Mouse.

'I will,' said Mole. 'And next year, I shall catch a leaf for you.'

32